Rey, Margret
  Curious George goes to
the circus.

Curious George®

GOES TO THE CIRCUS

Adapted from the Curious George film series
Edited by Margret Rey and Alan J. Shalleck

1 9 8 4
Houghton Mifflin Company Boston

Library of Congress Cataloging in Publication Data
Main entry under title:

Curious George goes to the circus.

"Adapted from the Curious George film series."
Summary: Curious George becomes the star of the
circus after he inadvertently gets in the way of the
acrobats' performance.
1. Children's stories, American. [1. Monkeys—
Fiction. 2. Circus—Fiction] I. Rey, Margret.
II. Shalleck, Alan J. III. Curious George goes to the
circus (Motion picture)
PZ7.C9218   1984   [E]   84-16826
ISBN 0-395-36636-4 (lib. bdg.)
ISBN 0-395-36630-3 (pbk.)

85B4775

Printed in Japan

10 9 8 7 6 5 4 3 2 1

"George," said the man with the yellow hat, "the
circus is in town tonight. Let's go."

At the circus lots of people were
standing in line for tickets.

"George," said the man, "I'm going to buy you some cotton candy. Wait right here and don't get into trouble."

While the usher was collecting the tickets,
George sneaked into the tent.

The acrobats had just climbed up to the platforms.

George was curious. Could he do that, too?
He grabbed the rope ladder and started to climb.

"Hey," called an acrobat. "Get off the ropes!
We've got to start our act."

But it was too late. The lights went out.
"THE WORLD'S GREATEST CIRCUS IS READY TO BEGIN,"
announced the ringmaster.

The lights came up again and an acrobat leaped into the net.

Another acrobat caught his partner in midair.

George wanted to get into the act.

He climbed to the top of the ladder and
onto the high platform.

Then he leaped into the air.

He bounced onto the net,

did a double somersault,

and finally landed on the ground.
The audience loved it.

But the acrobats were angry.
"He's stealing our act!" shouted one.
"That monkey's making a fool of us!" cried another.

George was scared.

He ran down the hall, where a long line of elephants
were getting ready for their act.

George climbed up the trunk of the last of the
elephants and hid behind his headdress.

The ringmaster was leading the elephants into the ring.

Suddenly, the last elephant raised his trunk

and let out an enormous sneeze.

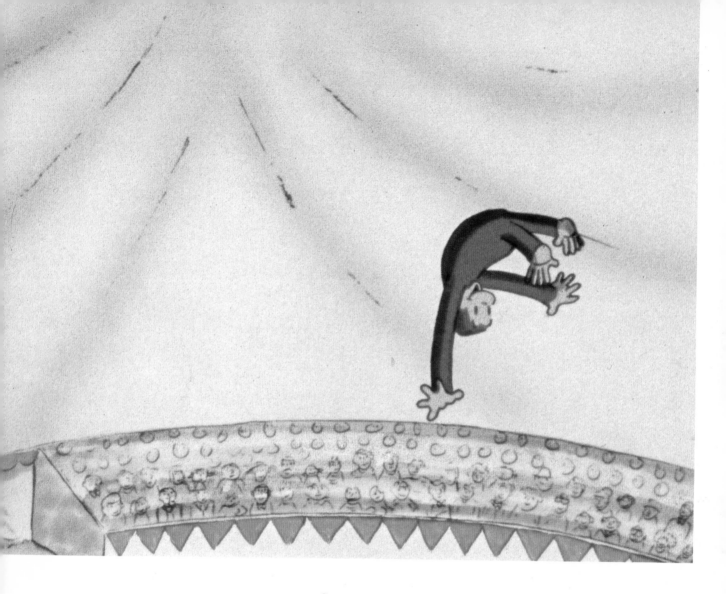

George flew through the air

and landed on the back of the first elephant.

The ringmaster was angry. "That's the monkey that messed up the acrobats' act," he shouted.

George kept riding around and around on
the elephant's back.

"Look!" cried a boy. "There's George! Isn't he great!" Everyone cheered.

"Well, George," said the ringmaster.
"You're forgiven for messing up the acrobats' act.
You were the star of the show."

"Three cheers for George!" they all shouted.